Ted and M

V

The Slugs

M A Macklin

Chapter 1

Don't eat 'the blue stuff'!

Ted and Mavis Fox, excited and raring to go, moved into number forty-nine Cedar Drive on the last day of April – perfect timing as they were both very keen gardeners; the soil was beginning to warm up ready for planting – it had been an exceptionally cold winter.

They used to enjoy telling their friends and neighbours that they loved, *'All God's creatures'*. "It's our job to feed and care for them, in fact I consider it an honour," Mavis would say, looking just a little too pleased with herself...

At the top of the garden, (just past the vegetable plot) were three beautiful cherry trees; in the spring their branches were heavy with pale pink blossom. It was here that the grey squirrels lived and thrived, their constant antics and acrobatics watched with admiration by this likeable middle-aged couple. Every spring the fat grey pigeons sat on the thinnest of the cherry tree branches determined to feast on the tasty young flowers. Sometimes, Ted and Mavis would run outside and clap their hands, making the pigeons fly away – but within minutes they had returned and more beautiful flowers were ripped to pieces.

"Never mind, Love, they mean no harm," Ted would say, smiling warmly at his wife. Early one morning as the bacon was sizzling in the pan, the couple looked out of the kitchen window, a vixen was hurrying through their garden – she looked tense and alert. Ted chuckled, "I expect she's come for breakfast, Mavis, that bacon does smell delicious – shall I fetch another plate?"

Ted's favourite magazine, 'Wildlife Weekly', had informed him that foxes love to eat eggs, so from that day forward, just as darkness was falling, Ted could be seen putting two extra-large eggs in front of the patio doors. Every morning he would find one empty eggshell on the lawn but the other egg was nowhere to be seen. No doubt it had been carried away in the fox's mouth – did she have cubs hidden nearby?

"No need to get those fancy, free range eggs, Mavis, far too expensive," declared Ted, "our fox won't care, will she? Remember what we always say? With our surname we're obliged to look after the foxes!"

Sadly, six weeks later, the eggs remained on the patio and their beautiful red fox failed to appear. "Cheer up, Ted, she'll return when she's hungry," said Mavis, reassuringly. "You never know, one day we might be lucky enough to see her cubs."

When Ted picked up the photo frame to admire their

'one and only' photograph of Freda the fox – it made him feel very sad. He sighed, "Oh, Mavis, do take a look, her coat is so thick and shiny – it must be all those lovely fresh eggs!"

Peanuts, sunflower seeds, stale bread (cut beautifully into tiny pieces) and other tasty left-overs were laid out for the birds to enjoy. Recently, a magnificent Victorian-style birdbath had been delivered; Mavis was so excited by the thought of it that she couldn't possibly sleep, longing for it to be used. Some people might have called it a monstrosity; it stood over a metre high and was decorated lavishly with cherubs, vine leaves and bunches of grapes. Even the stonework had been made to resemble marble – it would not have looked out of place standing in the gardens of a Roman villa. Once Mavis had spotted the birdbath on the internet, she had to have it. Being such a weighty item, the delivery alone cost thirty-five pounds. This year there would be no holiday in Cornwall for this caring couple, the birdbath had cost so much money, but they didn't mind – it was well worth the sacrifice...

Ted and Mavis couldn't resist spoiling their *'outdoor pets'* and it wasn't unusual for them to be seen wandering around the garden in their dressing gowns, long before the sun had made an appearance.

Despite this love of *'All God's creatures'*, Ted and Mavis thought it was perfectly acceptable to scatter poisonous 'blue pellets' onto the soil for the unloved, unwanted slugs to devour... Because the baby slugs rarely did as they were told, the following words had to be learned by heart – ASAP.

Here is the first lesson that every baby slug must learn: *'Never ever eat the little blue pellets that are scattered around by the big people'.*

Brothers Julian and Jeremy Slug had lived together in the garden of number forty-nine Cedar Drive for several years, long before the arrival of Ted and Mavis; these two elderly slugs were considered wise and reliable by all their friends and neighbours. They'd made a comfortable home beneath a thick leafy shrub where dead leaves could be gathered and brought inside. When Autumn arrived 'the boys' (as they were affectionately known), could lie back and enjoy the delicious smell of rotting leaves together with the odour and sliminess of damp and decay. No other slugs in the British Isles possessed such a splendid home...

Slugs are not fussy creatures but they do dislike the smell of garden flowers – especially jasmine, apple blossom, honeysuckle or rose petals; these 'heady fragrances' make them feel quite queasy.

On the day that the 'bright blue pellets' arrived, (scattered neatly under some very large leaves), many slugs had been tempted to devour them, greedily, despite being told that it was unwise to eat anything with which they were not familiar. They assumed that something so pretty, so blue, must be a very special treat, something yummy – hurray – at last the big people were starting to love them! Each and every slug who tasted this mystery food, whether young or old, met with a nasty and 'sticky' end. Didn't the big people know that the 'blue stuff' killed slugs? Why didn't they throw down something nice and tasty for them to eat? The big people enjoyed spoiling the foxes, the hedgehogs, the birds and even the naughty squirrels. Sometimes it felt as if nobody cared for them and it made them feel sad...

Slugs love things to be wet and muddy, so they were very fond of the tiny people, they were marvellous, they wandered around with little watering cans and frequently knocked over their drinks. Best of all, in the hot dry weather they splashed around in the large paddling pool until the lawn became soaking wet. The tiny people were messy eaters too – always dropping morsels of bread and cake which the slugs could enjoy, once the scary big people had gone back inside the bungalow. These much-admired tiny people were their heroes simply because they *never, ever,* scattered the dreaded 'blue stuff.'

This particular group of slugs, a variety known as 'Dusky' slugs considered themselves to be superior to the common variety, much prettier too with a bright orange stripe along their backs. It was easy for the silly snails to sneer at them, they had an easy life — they'd been blessed with a 'ready-made' house on their backs...

Chapter 2

A sneaky plan...

Slugs don't have arms or legs – they slide along on mucus which protects them from anything sharp. This large sociable group lived together in a shady, secret spot, right under the hostas where they could bury themselves beneath fallen leaves should it become too hot, *or* too cold.

Their leader made most of the decisions; his name was General Slug. He liked to shout and lay down the law, but nobody took much notice, after all, he was even older than 'the boys' and he was used to having his own way. Next year's birthday would be a very special one, The General would be six years old – assuming, of course, that he managed to avoid becoming a tasty meal for the terrifying blackbirds and thrushes with their sharp pointy beaks!

One warm, sunny evening in early summer, The General announced that there would be a 'special' meeting at the charming home belonging to Julian and Jeremy. Fresh damp leaves had been dragged inside, enabling everyone to relax and feel comfortable. Tasty, bright green shoots had been gathered up and laid out in a tidy pile. *"Don't wait to be asked, just help yourselves,"* insisted Julian, the perfect host – he'd always loved entertaining.

"Now then everyone, quiet please. I am calling this meeting as something has to be done about the 'blue stuff'." The General had an angry expression on his face, "Too many of the little ones are not listening to our warnings. Tonight, when the sky darkens, I shall go forth with 'the boys', we will search for a new home at the top of the garden, far, far away from the bungalow where the big people live. Yes, Julian, I'm well aware it will take all night to get there, but it has to be done."

After a light meal the three slugs set off, confidently, but very, very slowly. Many obstacles were encountered on their journey: bumpy and stony ground, tall matted grasses, tree roots and sharp gravel, but worst of all were the dreaded stinging nettles. Slugs are aware that during the dark hours, birds don't fly, they sleep in the branches; all would be well, there would be no swooping and whooshing noises, no huge scary shadows looming overhead.

For the slugs, the top of the garden was perfect, their very own Garden of Eden – but for the humans it was no more than a well-stocked vegetable patch. Julian and Jeremy felt happy and immensely proud of their leader. The General was feeling extremely pleased with himself too – saying to the boys, "I told you it would be worth the effort; now please remember, *we are here to look but not to eat.*"

There were signs of life in the vegetable patch: lettuce, spring greens, carrot tops, broad beans and beetroot; other healthy young plants caused excitement too.

"Stop right there!" shouted The General as Julian started to eat a tiny lettuce leaf. "I'll have none of that, we must leave no trace of tonight's visit. The big people must never know that we've been here, right to the very top of their precious garden." He sighed, "If our plan is to succeed, you *must* do exactly as I say."

"Come on then, follow me!" he bellowed. The boys slithered in behind The General, keeping close-by until they reached the cool, shady, wooded area. "Well, I told you we were in for a treat," said The General, "as you can see, I have saved the best 'til last... One of the slugs in next-door's garden told me about this place so come on chaps, have a good look round, it's just what we've been looking for! Here, in the dark wood, we can eat as much as we like, the big people will neither know nor care."

Many branches had been brought down by the wind, gathered up then left in a tidy pile by the big people. Long before they could see it, they could smell the tasty fungus;

it was growing in abundance on the rotting wood. The slugs were mystified by the shapes, sizes and colours: orange, beige, brown and pale cream. Every single variety tasted delicious. "Oh yes," whispered Jeremy, "bring it on! Do you know, I can hardly believe it, this fungus stuff smells even nicer than rotting Brussel-sprouts."

When they could eat no more, they decided to make their way home, which was anything but easy, on a full stomach…

Chapter 3

It's party time!

A few weeks later when the garden was at its finest, a message was passed around; *every slug,* young or old, would be expected to attend their monthly meeting. This time, as the subject was extremely important, they were asked to assemble at the ancient home belonging to The General and Mimi, his long-time partner. No excuses would be accepted...

Once everyone had settled down, (even the stragglers), The General began to speak – his booming voice could be heard for several metres. "I have a rather strange request but please don't worry, it will soon make sense... Tonight, I want you to gather in front of the bungalow. *We are going to party like never before!"*

The slugs looked very confused – what on earth was going on? This was not like The General, what was he playing at? He was an old 'stick-in-the-mud', he didn't *'do'* parties!

"You at the back, Sharon Slug, stop chatting and pay attention please, my plan is not as simple as it sounds. Right then, here goes: it's most important that we dance, skid, pirouette, perform figures of eight, make circles and keep active for as long as we can. Use your slimy slug trails, that's what they're for... It may sound harsh but I will allow you to sleep away the daylight hours only when you are absolutely exhausted – but not before..."

The General looked towards his eager band of followers. "Any question?" he asked. No-one said a word so he continued confidently, "The big people will assume that we have travelled down the garden and are now living very close to them – no doubt many more wretched blue pellets will be thrown down for us... When they see the enormous number of silvery trails covering their patio, they will think that there are hundreds, nay, thousands of us! They will go into panic mode!"

The slugs agreed that it was a brilliant plan and many of the tiny ones started to giggle. "Three cheers for The General!" shouted Mimi – everyone joined in...

For over a week, once the lights in the bungalow had been dimmed, the slugs carried out their clever plan. As expected, the silvery trails became very irritating and more than a little *embarrassing...* The big people were very angry, they didn't want slugs slithering all over their nice clean patio – whatever would the neighbours think?

"Now then, listen to me, you lot!" shouted The General, "I don't want to repeat myself, so concentrate, this is very important. In a week or so we shall be ready

to carry out 'stage two' of our cunning plan, therefore I need you to go home and relax, however, please keep doing your exercises, you'll need to be fighting fit..."

Chapter 4

A magnificent feast!

Their special day, their 'day of action', had arrived; the General referred to it as 'D Day'; the slugs were assembled and ready for their latest instructions. "Now then, the time has come for stage two of our plan," shouted The General, proudly. "I want everyone back here tonight – we will assemble outside the boys' home at midnight. *You at the back, Silvia Slug, are you giggling again? Any more silliness and you will be forced to live in next-door's garden; yes, I do know they have two dogs and three cats. Imagine having to slither through all that revolting 'mess'! No, you wouldn't like that very much!* Now, please remember, you must not eat anything today, I need you to set off with a very healthy appetite."

The Dusky slugs arrived at the vegetable patch at two forty-five in the morning – it had taken over two and a half hours to reach the top of the garden – a new record, beating their previous 'best time' by seven minutes. After such a mammoth trek, they were tired and very, very hungry

The night sky was pitch black with only a few distant stars to light their way, but that was a good thing it gave them a feeling of confidence – darkness had always been their friend...

"Please listen carefully," said The General. "Tonight, I want you to eat as much as you can; munch away to your heart's content, come back for seconds, thirds if you wish. We will not leave until we feel absolutely bloated." Hearing that, the young slugs started sniggering. "We must make sure the big people are thoroughly confused, they won't know where we live, or where to scatter the blue pellets. They will assume there are thousands of us and some have decided to move up here by the vegetable patch. However, their worst nightmare has just become a reality – even more slugs have arrived and they seemed determined to live close to the bungalow and make horrible, slimy, silvery trails all over the smart, clean patio."

The bright green lettuces and small savoy cabbages were particularly tasty, the tender young leaves enjoyed by one and all. The broad beans had been grown to perfection and now they were being devoured by 'the boys' who asked everyone to come over and join them for a taste of *'something special'*. The slugs enjoyed the broad beans so much that when they'd finished eating them, there remained no more than a few broken stalks and a handful of grubby beans laying on the muddy soil. Jeremy realized that if he wriggled around for a while, he could dislodge some of the baby new potatoes. "Anyone fancy a new potato?" he asked, excitedly, "they're soooo tasty!"

"I prefer my potatoes washed and peeled," replied Mimi; everyone fell about laughing when she attempted a 'posh' voice – trying hard to sound like one of the silly big people.

When they could eat no more, they set off for home, it took them far longer than they expected. Never before had the slugs enjoyed themselves so much or eaten such a magnificent feast.

Chapter 5

Copper tape and a nasty shock!

The following day The General declared that it was time for the girls to play their part. He needed two brave volunteers, two youngsters who would be prepared to slither and slide to the top of the garden in order to inspect the damage from the previous night. Flo and Jo, sitting at the back, were the first to offer their support. *"We'll do it, sir,"* they shouted, eagerly, *"please let us go with you, we're ever so brave..."*

Even before they had reached the top of the garden the trio of slugs were aware of raised voices – the big people sounded absolutely furious.

Ted and Mavis were standing in the middle of the vegetable patch, their faces red and angry. They hurled the remains of their precious vegetables towards the compost heap hoping that some of them might reach the target! "The little devils must have eaten ninety-per-cent of the stuff," shouted Ted, as he hurled a chewed-up cabbage right over his head. "I simply don't understand it, I thought the slugs had moved down to our end of the garden, right next to the bungalow – surely slugs can't be in two places at once, can they? Oh Mave, it's making my head spin – I don't think I can take much more of this..."

The other big person replied, ***"Oh no!*** I'd quite forgotten, it's this week your boss is coming for Sunday lunch, do you remember, I promised him and his wife some of our delicious home-grown broad beans, but there's hardly anything left, goodness me, whatever shall we do?"

Mavis paced up and down, her eyes fixed on their poor, shabby vegetable plot. Suddenly, a cheeky smile appeared upon her face. Taking a deep breath, she announced, "Ted, everything's going to be alright, no need to panic, I know what we can do! When we've finished here, we can go to the supermarket and buy some frozen broad beans – yes! We'll say they were grown in our very own vegetable plot. Your boss and his wife are 'townies', they'll never know the difference!"

Ted burst out laughing. "Oh, nice one Mave, well done girl – good thinking. You're so right, they couldn't possibly find out." Ted smiled, mischievously, "I bet they wouldn't know a broad bean from a Brussel sprout – specially with lots of delicious, rich gravy poured all over their roast dinner."

After sitting on the warm grass for several minutes, the tiny person felt obliged to speak up for the slugs. After a few moments, she said, ***"Uncle Ted, don't be so cross with the slugs – they get hungry too."*** Looking up at the big person she continued, "The slugs can't go to the supermarket, so why don't you make them their very own veg patch, then they might leave the big one alone? You look after me three days a week, when mummy is a work, so I can do all the watering."

"Do you know, that's not a bad idea, it might just work," said the big person, calming down a little. Later that day when Ted and Mavis walked out of the supermarket, they were carrying two bottles of red wine and a *very large bag of frozen broad beans.* A hasty visit to the garden centre had produced a roll of copper tape and packets of vegetable seeds. At this time of year, the seeds were half price so they grabbed several colourful packets, hardly bothering to look at what type of vegetables they might be.

The General and the girls had been keeping an eye on proceedings, they felt nervous, why were the big people always *so noisy, so shouty?* Nevertheless, they continued to watch from underneath the safety of a huge dandelion leaf, they dare not miss anything important...

Next to the compost heap was a small patch of uncultivated wasteland, the soil was poor and thin. The big people started to work on it; they tipped buckets of compost over the soil and began to dig it in. Next, they opened several packets of seeds and scattered them gently onto the soil. The tiny person was in charge of watering the seeds (which she did many times), back and forth until the ground was lovely and soggy.

Moving over to the vegetable plot, one of the big people, (the one with the loud voice), hammered in several stakes which were about twenty centimetres high – to these he attached a long roll of 'serrated' copper tape. The man who worked at the garden centre had laughed loudly when he advised Ted to buy the copper tape, saying, *"Cor, it's marvellous stuff, the blessed slugs and snails will receive a small electric shock if they touch it and they won't be back for another one – trust me. Look at it, mate, the top is serrated so it will cut the little devils too, yeah, serves 'em right!"* The little copper fence was placed all around Mavis and Ted's vegetable patch and it made the couple smile again. "Result!" whispered Ted.

After the big people had wandered back towards the bungalow, The General and the girls slithered over to find out what had been going on... The General watched as Flo and Jo (being fearless), decided to be the first to climb the lovely shiny copper fence. They wished they hadn't bothered – as soon as their slimy trails touched it, they received a small electric shock. "Oh, look at us!" squealed Flo – we're bleeding, too."

The serrated copper tape had scratched them in several places and a few drops of bright green slug-blood were visible – but the girls were okay. Yes, the copper tape worked very well, the man at the garden centre had said it would – he'd been so enthusiastic, so gleeful – so

20

mean...

"Never again," declared Flo and Jo Slug, they were frightened and very close to tears. This made The General feel guilty, perhaps *he* should have volunteered to climb the copper tape. "Let's keep to the *little* veg patch," said Flo, then she smiled, happily, "it looks perfect, doesn't it? It could have been made just for us... It will be so exciting when the green shoots start to show, I can't wait to go home and tell all the others!"

Chapter 6

All is not what it seems...

Ted and Mavis agreed that Sunday lunch with the boss and his wife had been a fantastic success. During the meal everyone agreed that the broad beans, (picked just hours earlier) from their very own garden, were the best they'd ever tasted – so much nicer than those awful frozen things. "Here's to the broad beans!" shouted the boss, as he raised his glass. Ted, Mavis and the boss's wife noticed that he struggled to stand up straight, he was more than a little wobbly... Everyone clinked their glasses together. Hooray! thought Ted, what a meal, what a day...

Feeling thirsty after such a large, delicious meal the boss's wife, Sheila, went into the kitchen for a glass of water. Being a kind and thoughtful person, she picked up the used paper napkins and walked over to the pedal bin. When she opened it, her heart started to race – on top of the potato peelings was a large green and white freezer bag. Smoothing out the creases, Sheila read the following words:

The Co-operative Store
Tender Young Broad Beans.
<u>**Keep Frozen**</u>
1.5 kg

At five o'clock, when their guests had left, Ted and Mavis relaxed with a well-earned cup of tea.

"Do you know, Mavis, I think there might be a pay rise on the horizon; we had such a laugh, didn't we? You never know, there could be an early promotion too. I don't want to go over the top but, let's just say, you'd better check out some holiday destinations – dust off the suitcases, we're on our way! Well done, you really did us proud – that meal went down a treat. *Specially our home-grown broad beans!"*

"Oh, Ted, you are a rascal," replied Mavis, who was looking very pleased with herself. "We got away with it, didn't we? That's the main thing..."

Chapter 7

Always tell the truth...

Reg and Sheila Griffin walked home slowly, they were so tired, due entirely to the amount of delicious food they'd consumed and maybe a little too much red wine. The boss's wife said to her husband, "Sorry love, but there's something I simply have to tell you, Ted Fox is not what he appears to be. Honestly Reg, I don't how I managed to keep quiet for the rest of the afternoon. What a pair of scoundrels, they made such a fuss about their 'perfect broad beans' even inviting us round to sample them, then, guess what? We're given the cheapo, frozen stuff! Perhaps they don't think we are good enough – what a nerve. Mind you, the frozen beans were quite tasty, I've had worse..."

Unfortunately for Ted and Mavis the pay rise was put on hold for a further year, the boss wasn't entirely sure that Ted Fox was a man to be trusted or that he was ready for promotion.

"I hope they don't invite us to their home again," said the boss, looking concerned. "They might, after all we had a really good time before we realized they don't always tell the truth. One thing's for sure – they will never know you looked inside the pedal bin and discovered that plastic bag, *no, never, not in a million years."*

"Did you noticed how they tried to steer us away from their vegetable plot?" continued Reg, narrowing his eyes, "Oh yeah, I thought it seemed a bit odd. Ted wanted to show off all the beautiful flowers and the miniature trees but never the vegetables..." Suddenly, Reg burst out laughing. *"Oh, my goodness, Sheila, did you see that birdbath? Who on earth do they think they are? Lord and Lady Muck?"*

"Yes," replied Sheila, sniggering, "of course I saw it, you could hardly miss it! Honestly, Reg, I didn't know where to look – it must have cost a fortune. I've never seen anything so elaborate in my life and I hope I never will again!"

The following day Reg and Sheila sat in their own small, neat back garden, enjoying a cup of tea and admiring the flowers. It wasn't large or showy but they loved it – it was their little place of safety after a hard day's work. They tried not to think about Ted and Mavis, they'd agreed never to mention them again, but it wasn't easy...

"Sheila – I've got a brilliant idea," said Reg, excitedly, "Why don't we invent a few 'ready-made' excuses, just in case we *do* get asked back?"

They laughed childishly as the 'excuses' were thought up, then written down on the back of an envelope – each one was given a number. At first, they sounded most convincing, but then the boss and his wife got rather carried away...

After her third cup of tea, Sheila was really getting into her stride. "How about this then?" she said to her husband. "If necessary, we could always send a text saying, '*Many thanks for the invitation, we'd love to come and see you, but...*

1. Reg has toothache – he's in agony.
2. Sheila has one of her migraines.
3. The washing machine has flooded the kitchen floor.

*It was then that the conversation started to get **very** silly and excuses were invented that they wouldn't dream of using!*

4. Reg fell off the ladder whilst cleaning out the guttering.
5. The dog has been sick on Sheila's lovely new dress.
6. The window cleaner locked us in the shed by mistake!
7. We have a plague of locusts in the garden.
8. We're not well, we might have caught 'Yellow Fever'.

"Oh, my goodness, I think that's enough for now, Reg. Do you know, I haven't laughed so much for ages? Ted and Mavis, huh – fancy telling such a great big lie. *I bet they've never planted any broad beans in their lives!*"

The slugs loved their new home, set midway between the fungus covered branches and the little veg patch. As soon as they moved in, Flo and Jo shouted, "Hooray for the tiny people!"

Under the watchful eye of The General, the slugs knew where it was safe to eat but more importantly the areas that must be avoided; the 'copper fence' was a barrier that no slug would be foolish enough to climb!

The tiny people looked after their own veg patch very seriously, it was watered and weeded regularly and they were already deciding what to plant next. Uncle Ted's gardening books were full of brightly coloured pictures, many displaying huge, prize-winning vegetables; some, like pumpkins and butternut squash, looked very interesting...

Never again were the dreaded 'little blue pellets' purchased or thrown down in the garden of number forty-nine – peace and harmony had at last been restored. Ted Fox knew exactly what was expected of him and his wife, after all, they considered it an 'honour' to look after their very own 'outdoor pets'; even the clever slugs deserved some respect...

The following Spring the shy, red vixen returned, bringing with her three fluffy, new-born cubs. The man in the village shop looked puzzled, he turned to his wife and whispered, "Look Sunita, over there, he's at it again! Why on earth does Ted Fox buy so many extra-large eggs? It's one of life's mysteries…"

The End